At the Side of
DAVID

By the same author:

At the Side of Esther
A Multiple-Ending Bible Adventure

At the Side of
DAVID

A Multiple-Ending
Bible Adventure

Written by
Eric Pakulak

Illustrated by
David Fielding

Pauline

BOOKS & MEDIA

Boston

Library of Congress Cataloging-in-Publication Data

Pakulak, Eric.
   At the Side of David : a multiple-ending Bible adventure /
writtenby Eric Pakulak ; illustrated by David Fielding.
       p. cm.
   Summary: As the fictional friend of David, King of Israel,
the reader makes decisions involving David's life.
   ISBN 0-8198-0768-0 (pbk.)
   1.   David, King of Israel—Juvenile fiction. 2.   Goliath,
(Biblical giant)—Juvenile fiction. 3.   Plot-your-own stories.
[1. David, King of Israel—Fiction. 2.   Goliath [Biblical
giant)—Fiction. 3. Plot-your-own stories.] I. Fielding,
David, 1946- ill. II. Title.
   PZ7.P174 As 2000
   [Fic]—dc21

00-008969

Translations of Psalms 23, 121, and an excerpt from Psalm 18
are taken from *The Contemporary English Version Bible,*
copyright © American Bible Society, 1995. Used with
permission.

Printed and published in the U.S.A. by Pauline Books & Media,
50 Saint Pauls Avenue, Boston, MA 02130-3491.

www.pauline.org

Pauline Books & Media is the publishing house of the
Daughters of St. Paul, an international congregation of women
religious serving the Church with the communications media.

1 2 3 4 5 6   05 04 03 02 01 00

For Mom and Dad,
whose love and support
mean more than
words can express

About This Book…

At the Side of David is based on the Bible's description of the life of David, Israel's great king.

As you read, you will enter into and *relive* his story as an *imaginary* friend. You'll even have your own choices to make.

The author and the publisher hope that interacting with this Bible story will help you to think about the values that led David to become one of the greatest heroes of the Jewish people.

A warm breeze rustles your hair as you sit under a tree overlooking a grassy meadow in the hills of Judah. You and your friend, whose name is David, are watching for Jesse, David's father.

As the sheep graze in the fields below, the air fills with beautiful music from David's harp. He sings:

> "You, Lord, are my shepherd.
> I will never be in need.
> You let me rest in fields of green grass.
> You lead me to streams of peaceful water,
> and you refresh my life.
>
> "You are true to your name,
> and you lead me along the right paths.
> I may walk through valleys as dark as
> death,
> but I won't be afraid.
> You are with me,
> and your shepherd's rod makes me feel
> safe.

"You treat me to a feast,
while my enemies watch.
You honor me as your guest,
and you fill my cup until it overflows.

"Your kindness and love
will always be with me
each day of my life,
and I will live forever
in your house, Lord."

"That's beautiful, David," you say.

"Thank you," he replies.

David plays some other songs that he's written as you sit back and enjoy the peacefulness of the spring afternoon.

Suddenly, a stirring in the bushes behind you interrupts the music. Though you are alarmed at first, you soon find that the noise is just the approach of a messenger from the town of Bethlehem.

"I've been sent by Jesse," says the messenger, "to summon David back to town."

After you assure David that you can watch the sheep by yourself, he and the messenger head for Bethlehem.

Throughout the afternoon you wonder why David was suddenly called from the fields. As it gets later, you begin to worry. You feel really relieved when you finally see David's familiar figure running toward you.

"The Lord has chosen me to be the next king of Israel!" he exclaims as he sits down beside you.

"I can't believe it! What great news!" you almost shout.

David tells you about how Samuel, one of God's prophets, filled his heart with the Spirit of the Lord by pouring oil over his head. He also explains that he won't become king until Saul, the present king, dies.

In spite of the wonderful news, your lives soon return to normal. The peaceful routine of watching the sheep in the fields continues until one day another messenger, this time dressed in an Israelite uniform, arrives.

"The great King Saul of Israel wishes David, son of Jesse, to come to the palace and play the harp for him in times of sadness," he announces.

"I must go," David tells you. "If you'd like to, I would be happy to have you come with me to live at the palace. But I understand if you don't want to leave your family."

If you go with David to the palace, turn to page 11.

If not, turn to page 13.

"I'd be honored to come and live with you at the palace of King Saul," you tell David.

"Great!" he exclaims.

Soon enough, King Saul appoints you as an assistant to David.

For weeks, you and David enjoy an easy life. David plays his harp and soothes Saul's heart whenever the king feels sad. When the king is in a better mood, the two of you relax and do a few odd jobs around the palace.

One day, King Saul calls all his people together. "Our enemies, the Philistines, have once again invaded Judah," he says. "It's time for me to lead our armies to war."

When King Saul goes off to battle, you and David return to Bethlehem. It's not long before you are back to your old job of watching sheep.

One evening, you're having supper with David and his family after a day in the fields. Jesse, David's father, hands David a sack. "Here are ten loaves of bread and a bushel of grain," he says. "Take them to your three eldest brothers who are fighting with the Israelite army."

"I'll need someone to watch the sheep," David tells you. "But if you'd rather come with me to check on my brothers, I can find someone else."

If you want to watch the sheep, turn to page 13.

If you'd rather accompany David, turn to page 14.

"I'll stay here and take care of the sheep," you say. "But I'll think of you and pray for you every day."

"All right," says David. "I hope to see you soon. May the Lord be with you."

With that, David leaves Bethlehem, and you continue with your work as a shepherd.

For a while everything is fine. Then one day a sheep tumbles down a steep hill and gets trapped inside a ditch.

Quickly, you take your staff and follow the animal's frantic cries. You finally spot the sheep about twenty feet below you. It looks like you can make it down. Slowly, carefully, you make your way to the base of the hill. You pick up the frightened sheep. Then, just as you're beginning to climb back up, you see something out of the corner of your eye. When you turn to investigate, you're shocked. There, about one hundred yards away, in a small forest, is a Philistine army camp!

"Halt!" yells a soldier.

If you try to run back up the hill, turn to page 18.

If you do as the soldier says, turn to page 19.

"I'd like to come with you," you tell David.

"Good," he replies. "I'll get someone else to watch the sheep."

It doesn't take long to find someone else to look after the flocks. You both get a good night's sleep and leave for the Israelite army camp at daybreak.

When you finally arrive at the camp, the army is preparing for battle. You follow David as he makes his way to the front where his brothers are. Suddenly, as David is giving his brothers news from home, a man who is at least nine feet tall comes forward from the ranks of the Philistine army, which is now directly opposite the Israelite army.

"It's the giant! The giant Goliath has returned!" yell some Israelite soldiers in fear.

Then, in the mightiest voice you've ever heard, the giant shouts, "I defy the Israelite army! Send a man to fight me!"

"Who is this Philistine to defy the armies of the living God?" David cries. "I'll fight him with the help of God!"

Hearing this, a group of soldiers run back to a large orange tent where you presume King Saul is. Soon David is called to the same tent where he seems to have persuaded King Saul to let him fight Goliath.

"God will help me to overcome him," says David as he runs toward Goliath with only a sling-shot in his hand.

Even though Goliath laughs at David because he's only a boy, you have no doubt that David will win with the Lord on his side.

Sure enough, David is able to knock Goliath down with a single stone from his sling. Next he beheads him with the giant's own sword.

With the death of their giant, the Philistine army quickly retreats, followed by the victorious Israelites.

After the slaying of Goliath, King Saul is very pleased with David. He's so pleased that he soon names him captain of his army. You become David's top assistant as he leads the Israelite army on to many victories.

One day, as you come back from yet another victory over the Philistines, some women begin singing a song that makes King Saul very jealous of David. They sing, "Saul has slain his thousands and David his ten thousands."

The next day, when you accompany David to play the harp for Saul, the king seems more troubled than usual. Without warning, in the middle of a beautiful song, King Saul throws his spear at David. *How dare he!* David escapes from

the room, but you still sit across from Saul, staring at the spear in front of you.

If you throw the spear back at Saul, turn to page 26.

If you resist the temptation for revenge and follow David, turn to page 27.

You quickly begin to climb back up the steep hill. Within moments, arrows are hitting the ground all around you.

The Philistines aren't cruel enough to kill an innocent, defenseless person, you tell yourself.

But in a matter of seconds a soldier is in front of you, his arrow is aimed and ready to fire…

The End

The soldier's tone of voice tells you that it would be wise to do as he commands. You slowly put down the sheep and raise your hands above your head. The soldier takes you to the Philistine camp.

"This fine young shepherd will make a good assistant to the doctors in our army," he announces to the others.

You are given a cloak with the Philistine emblem on it and are lead to a small tent. There you meet an old man who appears to be the head doctor.

"Follow my orders," he tells you.

Immediately you begin helping to care for the injured Philistine soldiers. You continue to do this for several days. Then one day the captain of the army calls everyone together.

"Tomorrow at sunrise," he says, "we'll travel back into Philistia. There we'll join more of our men for an attack on Israel."

"Why do they need our help?" someone asks. "They have the giant, Goliath."

"Haven't you heard?" the captain says. "Goliath was slain by a young boy named David."

David! You think. *I can't go with them to fight against my best friend!*

Later you ask the captain, "May I leave now?"

"Of course not!" he answers. "You're now a member of the Philistine army."

You feel very unhappy that you can't return to your family and friends. But you also know that it is impossible to escape. The Philistine camp is heavily guarded both day and night.

Early the next morning you help to break up camp. Soon you're on the march with the army. Before noon, the troop you're traveling with meets four more regiments. You join forces and head back toward Judah. There you come to a large plateau. The Israelite army stands ready on the other side.

"Charge!" the army captains shout, as soldiers from both armies run toward each other. When the fighting begins, you and the others who assist the doctors set up tents where you will provide medical help for the wounded.

As the fighting draws nearer, a desperate soldier stumbles into the medical camp. "They've broken through our defense!" he screams. "Run for your lives!"

You hear a loud shriek as an Israelite's arrow strikes down a soldier. Everything is chaos now. You race from the tent. In a panic, you see three armed Israelites coming toward you. Behind them is another soldier, wearing a captain's helmet. His face is strangely familiar. As the men get closer and draw their bows and arrows, you realize that the face under the captain's helmet is David's!

If you run for your life and try to contact David later, turn to page 22.

If you stay where you are and hope that David recognizes you, turn to page 23.

You're desperate for David to recognize you, but there's no time to talk. You follow the others from your tent as they run for cover. Israelite arrows are whizzing by you. Looking back, you see that David is one of the archers who is firing in your direction.

If only he knew! you think.

Suddenly, as you're still looking back, you trip and fall to the ground. Frantically you yell, "Stop! David! It's…" But it's too late. An arrow sends you home to the Lord.

The End

You tear off your Philistine cloak and sink to your knees, yelling, "Stop, David! It's me, your best friend, not a Philistine!"

As one of the Israelite soldiers prepares to throw his spear at you, you pray that David has heard you.

"Is it *really* you?" he asks as he comes closer.

"Yes! Yes!" you gasp.

David throws his strong arms around you, saying, "I can't believe it! How did you ever end up here?"

"Let's get away from here and I'll tell you all about it," you promise.

"Yes. I've done my share of fighting today," David says. "Follow me."

He leads you away from the battlefield and into an Israelite tent. There you tell him your incredible story.

"Thank God you were able to survive and find me!" David exclaims at the end.

"And I heard," you say, "that you killed the Philistine giant all by yourself. Is it true?"

David nods. "I was taking some bread to my brothers who were fighting in this very same army," he explains, "and this giant appeared and defied the armies of God. So, with the Lord's help, I slew him. After that King Saul was very pleased with me, so pleased in fact, that he made me a captain in his army."

But David looks sad and confused as he tells you the rest of his story. "After I returned from my first big victory over the Philistines, some women sang that Saul had slain his thousands and me, my ten thousands. This made Saul very jealous. He even tried to attack me with his spear one day." David shakes his head. "I escaped uninjured," he adds, "but now I must return to the palace, and I don't know what to expect from King Saul."

With that, David and the other captains round up their troops and you join the victorious Israelite army on its march back to the palace.

Turn to page 28.

In a fit of anger, you pull the spear out of the wall and throw it at Saul with all your might. Though it's a good throw, the king is able to avoid it and shouts for his guards.

"How dare you attack David!" you shout. "He's never done a thing to harm you!"

Still angry, you rush at the king. But, before you can get to him, two Israelite guards burst into the room. Suddenly, you're a prisoner....

The End

You're able to race out of the room before Saul tries to harm you, too.

"Whew!" you gasp. "That was close!"

"*Too* close," David replies.

Turn to page 28.

The next day, David has someone he wants you to meet.

"This is Jonathan," he says. "He's King Saul's son and a good friend of mine."

Jonathan smiles, and you soon become friends.

All three of you wait patiently during the next few days to see what Saul will do next. The suspense is finally broken when Saul calls for David.

"Saul has promised me the hand of Michal, his daughter, if I kill one hundred Philistines," says David when he returns unharmed. "Because I've fallen in love with her, I will leave tomorrow with one thousand soldiers."

"This is just another attempt to kill you," you warn. "Only this time, Saul is using the Philistines instead of his own hand."

"Even if it is another attempt," David replies, "I have the Lord to protect me."

Sure enough, David slays one hundred Philistines the next day and soon has Michal as his wife.

Over the next few weeks, Saul makes a few more attempts on David's life. He even tries to get Jonathan to kill him. Even though Jonathan is able to calm Saul down for a while, talking him out of his evil plan, the danger soon becomes too great. You and David must escape to the prophet Samuel's house, where you hide for a time.

"We can't hide forever," David tells you one day. "We have to go to see Jonathan."

Soon you both sneak back to the palace where you are able to talk to Jonathan secretly.

"What do you want me to do?" he asks.

"There will be a new moon tomorrow," David explains. "Your father always invited me for a meal at the time of the new moon. I won't come tomorrow. Tell him I had to go to Bethlehem. If he doesn't mind, that means it's safe for me to return. If he's angry, he will still want to kill me."

Now David turns to you. "You've always come with me to Saul's dinner at the new moon," he says. "Would you rather go to the meal with Jonathan or stay here with me?"

If you go with Jonathan, turn to page 30.

If you stay with David, turn to page 43.

"I think it would be better if I went with Jonathan," you answer.

"All right," says David.

After a code is worked out to let David know whether Saul plans to kill him or not, you say good-bye and head for the palace with Jonathan.

On the first day of the new moon, you and Jonathan take your usual places at the king's table. Though it's obvious that David is missing, Saul says nothing.

However, on the second day Saul asks, "Where is David?"

"He asked permission to return to Bethlehem for a few days," Jonathan replies, "because his family offers a sacrifice every year at this time."

Saul flies into a rage in front of everyone. "Bring David back at once!" he thunders at Jonathan. "He shall die!"

"But why do you want to kill him?" Jonathan protests. "He's never done anything to harm you."

Saul's face turns red and his eyes flash in anger. He jumps up and throws his spear at his own son! Jonathan is so shaken that he goes to his room.

Later, you visit him. "Tomorrow morning I'll go to the fields and warn David," he tells you. "I think it would look suspicious if you went with me. Maybe you should stay here."

"Yes, you're right," you answer. "I'll stay."

The next morning, after Jonathan has already left, a servant informs you that King Saul wants to see you.

What could he want with me? you wonder as you walk to Saul's room.

"I've been watching you," the king says, "and I feel you would make a good assistant. Do you accept?"

If you accept Saul's offer, turn to page 32.

If not, turn to page 36.

"I would be honored to serve the king of Israel," you respond.

"Good," replies Saul. "I will be glad to have you."

Soon you are at Saul's side almost all the time, giving him advice and helping him to keep his temper.

One day Saul receives a message. Immediately after reading it, he begins to call the army together.

"What is it?" you ask.

"I've just received word on where David is hiding," Saul explains. "Now I'll go kill him!"

You don't want to hunt your best friend, but Saul insists that you go. You're given a bow and arrows just in case, although Saul promises that you won't have to fight.

Soon you reach a thick forest where David is supposed to be hiding. Saul has the area almost completely surrounded by Israelite soldiers.

Suddenly a soldier runs up to Saul. "I've found David," he says. "He's hiding in a field of large underbrush not three hundred feet from where we're standing."

Hearing this, Saul takes ten of his best soldiers to attend him as he goes to kill David himself. After Saul leaves, you hurry to find a spot where you can see your friend. When you finally find one, Saul is just thirty feet from David, who doesn't see him. Even though you are Saul's assistant, you know that you must try to save David.

If you shoot at Saul, turn to page 34.

If you shout to David, turn to page 35.

As quietly as possible, so as not to alert the Israelite soldiers, you crawl to a place where you can get a good shot at the king. As Saul continues to sneak closer to David, you draw back your bow and arrow, aim carefully, and fire. Though on target, the shot is weak, and your arrow bounces off the armor covering Saul's shoulder. The king's soldiers rush toward Saul to see if he's been injured. The commotion alerts David and his men of the danger.

"The arrow came from back there!" cries one of the king's soldiers. You dive into some bushes before they see you.

Turn to page 40.

"David!" you shout. "Look out!"

Hearing this, David turns around to see Saul and his soldiers approaching. He crawls deeper into the bushes. As David's men recognize the danger, they too spring into action. You have no time to watch what's happening. A few Israelite soldiers are now after you!

With the soldiers in pursuit, you're almost run over by a messenger on horseback. He calls out for Saul. "The Philistines have invaded our country!" he shouts. "Hurry!"

This will definitely save David, you think. *I must find a way to get to him.* But you never get the chance. The messenger has slowed you just enough that the soldiers are now upon you...

The End

"Thank you anyway," you say, "but I don't think so."

"If you refuse to be loyal and to serve your king," Saul bellows, "then I'll leave you out in the wilderness to starve!"

You're now under house arrest and no longer allowed out of your room. Late one night, a whisper wakens you. "Psssst," you hear. "It's me, Jonathan."

"Jonathan?" you whisper back. "Thank God!"

"I've heard about my father's plans," he tells you. "I found out where he's going to leave you, and I've hidden some food and supplies nearby. Near the supplies, you'll see a small trail. Follow it until you get to a road. This is the way David went."

"Thank you, Jonathan," you sigh in relief.

"You're welcome," he whispers. "Now I must leave."

The next morning you're led deep into the wilderness, and the guards leave you. It doesn't take you very long to find the supplies left by Jonathan: enough food and drink for three days and some warm clothes. You're able to find the trail that Jonathan mentioned and you eventually get to the road, which takes you to a small town.

"Which way did he go?" you ask some people who say they saw David.

"He said that he was headed for the land of Judah," they reply.

After resting for a while, you leave for Judah, your homeland. Though it's a long, hard trip, you're anxious to see your family again. When you arrive in Judah, you find that David has already gone elsewhere. You continue on to Bethlehem. Your family is overjoyed to see you and hear all about your adventures. After you've shared all your news, you find out that David's family left Bethlehem to join him just a week before your arrival.

If you continue to try to catch up with David, turn to page 39.

If you stay with your family and live in Bethlehem for a while, turn to page 45.

After spending a few more days with your family, you pack up some supplies and head back the way you came in search of David. On your way out of Judah, you ask a few people in each village if they have seen or heard of David.

"He's hiding in a nearby forest," says one man, "and I've heard that Saul knows his whereabouts and is coming to get him."

At first, you think this must be a rumor, but then you hear it repeated so many times along your way, you decide to find out for yourself. Not too long after, you're walking along a trail through the forest. As you go deeper into the dark woods, you begin to hear noises. Soon you can make out figures and shapes. As you get closer still, you recognize Israelite soldiers!

They must have David surrounded! you think.

You're able to find a hiding place very near to the Israelite camp. From there, you can see that Saul has crept up behind the large rocks where David is hiding—unaware of the king's presence.

If you shout a warning to David, turn to page 35.

If you try to crawl through the bushes to David, turn to page 40.

Just as a few soldiers begin searching the bushes you're crawling through, an Israelite messenger comes riding through the forest shouting, "Hurry! The Philistines have invaded our country!"

You lie absolutely still as the Israelites quickly pull out of the forest. After making sure that they've all gone, you run up to David.

"David!" you cry. "I've been searching all over for you!"

Your friend is as overjoyed to see you as you are to see him. But David reminds you that he must find another hiding place because he's still in danger. You also learn that about four hundred men are now following David.

Soon, you, your best friend, and his men are on your way to Engedi, a wild, rocky country near the Dead Sea. Along the way, you exchange stories with David. He tells you how he pretended to be crazy to escape the Philistine king. You also find out that his family was taken to a safe place in the land of Moab so Saul couldn't harm them.

"We'll hide in this cave for a while," David says when you finally reach your destination.

After a long time, there is some noise and movement outside. Soon a man enters the cave to rest briefly and to take care of his needs. To everyone's surprise, it's none other than Saul!

"God has given you a chance to kill your enemy," some men begin to whisper to David.

Without saying a word, David quietly creeps up and cuts off a piece of Saul's cloak. When Saul leaves the cave, David follows him out. "My lord, the king!" he calls loudly.

Saul is startled and turns around.

"Why do you believe those who say I'm trying to harm you?" David asks. "Look!" he cries, as he holds up the piece of Saul's cloak for him to see. "Since I just cut off a piece of your cloak and didn't kill you, even though I had the chance, believe that I don't want to hurt you!"

Saul begins to cry. "You're right and I'm wrong," he tells David. Then Saul and his men leave for home.

"I don't trust Saul," David says after they leave. "We must keep moving."

With that, you, David, and all his men head for the desert of Maon, which is south of the Dead Sea. By the time you reach the land owned by Nabal, a very rich farmer, the men are getting hungry because they've run out of food.

"Why don't we steal a few of Nabal's sheep?" the men suggest.

"No," says David.

Instead, he sends messengers to Nabal asking for some food. But the stingy farmer refuses to give any food to David and is rude to his messengers.

"Prepare to go and punish Nabal," David commands his men.

However, before they have a chance to leave, a group of donkeys, loaded down with food and wine, appear. Before anyone can say a thing, a woman approaches from behind the donkeys and introduces herself as Abigail, Nabal's wife. She apologizes for her husband's behavior and offers the food that she has brought. David is so impressed with Abigail that, when Nabal dies ten days later from a sickness sent by God, David marries her.

Turn to page 52.

"I'll stay here with you," you answer.

"After I learn my father's intentions," says Jonathan, "I'll come to the field to practice shooting my bow and arrow. If I tell my servant boy that the arrows are on this side, it means everything is safe. But, if I say that the arrows are beyond him, it means my father is still not friendly toward you."

With that, Jonathan leaves for the palace. You and David wait quietly for two days. Then, on the morning of the third day, Jonathan appears with a boy to fetch his arrows.

"The arrow is farther on, beyond you," shouts Jonathan after he shoots an arrow over the boy's head.

After shooting for a little while longer, Jonathan gives the boy his bow and tells him to take it back to the city. When the boy is gone, you and David come out of your hiding place and say a tearful good-bye to Jonathan.

To escape from Saul, you and David now decide to go to Gath in the land of the Philistines. However, people recognize David as a captain in the Israelite army and he is brought before the king. Thankfully, he's able to escape by pretending to be insane.

Since Gath isn't safe, the two of you return to Judah, where you hide in a large cave. In a few days,

David's family also comes down to the cave to hide from Saul.

Soon many Israelites who don't like Saul begin to join David. Before long, there are four hundred men.

"We must find a new hiding place," says David to his men.

Later, when the two of you are alone, he tells you, "While we're close to Bethlehem, I thought you might want to go back and live with your family for a while. It's up to you."

If you decide to return to your family, turn to page 45.

If you don't want to leave David yet, turn to page 46.

Your family is very happy that you've decided to stay, and you go back to your usual farm work.

For a long time, you hear no news from or about David. Then one day you find out that Saul and three of his sons, including Jonathan, have been killed in battle. Even though you're very sad about the death of your friend Jonathan, you're happy that David will now become king.

In a couple of days, you receive a message inviting you to the ceremony in the city of Hebron during which David will be anointed king of Israel. After this exciting event is over, David asks to speak with you privately.

"I'd like to have you come to live at the palace with me as my assistant," he says.

If you accept David's offer, turn to page 57.

If you would rather continue living with your family, turn to page 56.

"I'd like to come with you," you tell David.

"Good," he replies. "I'm glad to have you at my side."

With that, David leads his four hundred men to a city in the land of Moab, where he arranges a safe place for his family to hide from King Saul. However, a prophet soon comes to David and tells him that God wishes him to return to Judah.

When you arrive back in the land of Judah, David finds a dense forest where all of you hide from Saul. However, the king soon learns where David is and comes to get him. For many days, you are chased throughout the land, once escaping only because Saul has to leave quickly to defend Israel against the Philistines.

After such a close call, David leads his men to Engedi, a wild and rocky country near the Dead Sea. There you find a large cave in which all the men will fit without being seen. Suddenly, as you sit quietly in the darkness, a man enters the cave to take care of his needs. When you take a closer look, you realize that the man is Saul!

"God has given you a chance to kill your enemy," whisper the men to David.

But, instead of killing him, David cuts off a piece of the king's cloak. When Saul leaves the cave, David follows him out. He shows the king the piece

of cloak, pointing out that he didn't kill him even though he had the chance. This shames Saul so much that he promises to leave David alone for good.

"I don't trust Saul," David confides, "so we'll travel south to the desert of Maon."

On your way there, you pass through the land of a very rich man named Nabal. Because the now nearly six hundred men are getting hungry, David sends some messengers to ask Nabal for food.

The messengers return to tell David how rudely Nabal treated them before sending them away with no food.

"Prepare to go and punish this stingy man," David tells his men.

But, before they have a chance to leave, a donkey appears. Taking a closer look, you find that it is loaded down with food and wine—and that there are four more behind it!

A woman quickly dismounts one of the donkeys and approaches David.

"I am Abigail, Nabal's wife," she says, "and I want to apologize for his rudeness."

Later, when Abigail has gone, David tells you that he is very impressed with her. Ten days later, as though punished by God, Nabal gets sick and dies.

"Now I can ask Abigail to marry me," David tells you. "Would you like to bring my marriage proposal to her?"

If you would, turn to page 50.

If not, turn to page 51.

"I'd be happy to," you say.

Within an hour, you are standing at the front door of a magnificent farmhouse. "May I speak with Abigail, please?" you ask the servant who comes to the door.

"My good friend, David," you explain to Abigail when she arrives, "would like very much to marry you. Will you come with me?"

"It would be an honor to marry David," Abigail replies, "but who will take care of the farm?"

"I'll take care of the farm for you," you offer. "You won't have to worry."

"Thank you!" exclaims Abigail.

After giving you detailed instructions about the farm, she leaves to marry your best friend.

For a long time, you enjoy the peaceful life of the country. Then one day you find out that Saul has died and David has become king. Though he offers to make you one of his close assistants, you choose to continue overseeing Abigail's farm. Upon Abigail's death a few years later, you inherit the large estate. In the years after that, you marry, have children, and then grandchildren, all of whom enjoy the stories you tell about your famous friend David.

The End

"No, thank you," you reply, "I'd prefer not to."

"All right," he says. "I'll send someone else."

With that, David promptly sends another messenger to propose to Abigail. When the messenger returns with her, everyone rejoices because Abigail has agreed to marry David.

Turn to page 52.

After the wedding, David leads you and the rest of his men deep into a forest where you set up camp. For a while you live in peace there. But, just as David begins to think that Saul is actually keeping his promise to leave him unharmed, some spies bring upsetting news. King Saul is heading your way with a large army!

One night, David leaves you in charge of the men and he takes his chief soldier with him to try to locate Saul's camp. After about an hour, he returns.

"What happened?" you ask anxiously.

"We found Saul," he answers. "He was asleep. Beside his head were a spear and a pitcher of water. Rather than killing him, I awakened Abner, Saul's general. Abner then alerted the king," David continues. "When Saul saw that I had spared his life again, he apologized and promised not to harm me."

"But he can't be trusted," you insist.

"I know," David agrees. "That's why we must leave this country and hide in the land of the Philistines."

With that, David leads his six hundred men toward Philistine country. Along the way, a few high-ranking Israelite soldiers join your group and become captains over the men.

Upon your arrival, the king of the Philistines gives David the town of Ziklag to hide in. For over a year everyone lives there peacefully. Then one day David receives word that the Philistines are preparing to go to war against the Israelites. Immediately, you go with David and his men to the Philistine king and offer to help him. But the king doesn't accept your offer, because some of the other Philistine leaders are afraid that David might turn against them in battle.

When you return to Ziklag, everyone is shocked to find that some wandering Amalekites have burned down the city and have taken the wives and children.

"The Lord has told me to pursue the Amalekites," David says later. Soon he goes with four hundred men and leaves you in charge of the town.

Things go as smoothly for you in Ziklag as they do for David, who soon returns with all the wives and children.

"I wonder how the battle between the Israelites and the Philistines is going?" David says.

In two days, David's question is answered. A young man, whose clothes are dirty and torn, comes running into town.

"I've just escaped from the Israelite camps," he pants. "The Philistines have conquered…and Saul and his son Jonathan are dead!" He holds out his trembling hands to David. "I give these to you… King Saul's crown and bracelet."

For the rest of the evening everyone mourns and fasts in memory of Saul, Jonathan, and all of the Israelite soldiers who have died.

"The Lord has told me," David announces the next day, "to go to Hebron to be anointed king."

With that, you, David, and all of his followers make the journey to Hebron. People from all over Israel are already pouring into the city by the thousands to show their loyalty to David. In a few days, your best friend is proclaimed king of Israel before a huge crowd.

"I would like you to remain with me as my personal assistant," David tells you later. "But, if you'd rather settle down elsewhere, I'll understand."

If you become David's assistant, turn to page 57.

If not, turn to page 56.

"I think that I'll return to Bethlehem and try to start a family of my own," you tell David, "but I'll keep in contact and pray for you every day."

"I'll pray for you, too," David promises. "Good luck, my friend."

Though it's hard to leave David, you just feel that there's a wonderful life waiting for you at home. And you are right.

Within a year after settling in Bethlehem, you are married, and eventually you have five children. They enjoy hearing over and over again the stories about your famous friend, David, king of Israel.

The End

"I would be honored to help you in any way I can," you tell David.

"Wonderful!" he replies. "I'm also honored to have you at my side."

After David's anointing, time passes quickly. Within seven years, the royal city is moved from Hebron to Jerusalem, which is easier to defend in case of war.

One day, about a year after moving to Jerusalem, David calls for a meeting of his chief advisors. "I've been thinking," he says, "that the golden ark of the Lord is still in Kiriath-jearim, where it has been since the Philistines captured it twenty years ago. I think we should return it to Jerusalem."

Everyone agrees that this is a wonderful idea and soon David is leading his people in a long parade to Kiriath-jearim. When you arrive there, the ark is placed on a cart that is headed back toward Jerusalem with much singing and dancing.

As you near Jerusalem with the ark, something very unexpected happens. You come across some rough, uneven ground and the ark almost falls off the cart. Uzzah, one of the drivers, reaches out to steady the ark. But, as soon as he touches it, he falls dead on the spot. This frightens everyone so much that David has the ark placed in a nearby house for a while. Three months later, when David sees how much the Lord has blessed the family that kept the ark, he gives orders to move it to Jerusalem.

This time, with the Levites carrying the ark on their shoulders as Moses commanded, it is brought safely into Jerusalem.

Upon its arrival, the ark is placed in a tent that has been specially set up for it.

One day, David comes to talk to you. "I've been thinking," he says. "We live in a beautiful house while the Lord's holy ark sits in a tent." He goes on to tell you of his plan to build a beautiful temple for the ark. David also tells the prophet Nathan about his plan. Nathan is very pleased and shares the idea with God.

Then Nathan reports to David, "Because your life has been so full of war, the Lord wishes the temple to be built by your son who will become king after you."

Even though he wanted to build the temple himself, David is happy to hear this news. He soon begins preparing everything for his son to build a beautiful temple.

Some months later, David receives word that King Nahash of Ammon, a nearby country, has died. As a thoughtful gesture, David has you lead a group of messengers to bring words of comfort to Hanun, Nahash's son.

When you arrive in Ammon, you are taken straight to King Hanun. As you enter the large room where Hanun sits on his throne, you notice the strange tension in the air. Suddenly the king yells, "Seize them!" and the palace guards charge at you. Somehow, in all the confusion, you're able to slip by the guards and jump through a small window to the ground below. No one has seen your escape, and you run into the forest that surrounds the palace.

After wandering through the woods for an hour, you come upon a trail. Investigating further, you find that it leads to a small, run down shack, which seems to have been abandoned long ago. You enter the shack to sit down and rest a little, but you are more tired than you realize and you soon fall into a deep sleep…

You finally wake up to the sound of voices outside. "We must hurry and tell King Hanun," someone is saying, "that King David of Israel has sent an army to avenge our treatment of his messengers."

What happened to the rest of my men? you wonder. But you have no time to think…. David's soldiers are on their way to begin a battle and you could be caught in the middle!

If you stay in the shack until the fighting is over, turn to page 61.

If you want to leave the shack and try to reach David's army, turn to page 62.

You quickly decide that it would be best to hide in the woods until the battle is over. You gather all the nuts and berries you can find and store them in the shack. You also do your best to barricade your hideout in case enemy soldiers find it. Now all you can do is wait.

For two weeks, you live quietly in the secluded shack and your only visitors are a few friendly animals from the woods. But one day, as you're out gathering more food, you hear in the distance what sounds like an army approaching. Though you're not sure whose army it is, you take no chances and return to your hideout.

As the soldiers move closer, you find that your worst nightmare has come true—it's the enemy! You do your best to be quiet, but your hideout is found by the troop of tired soldiers. They're searching for a resting-place, and your shack looks inviting. They break through your makeshift barricade and discover you within minutes. Though you plead with them, they recognize you as a foreigner and take you prisoner…. It will be up to King Hanun to decide what to do with you now.

The End

You leave the shack and head back toward Israel as quickly as possible. After traveling for most of the day, you find a dry cave and decide to settle down for the night. Though you are awakened a few times by the noise of some small forest animals, you make it safely through the night. After a breakfast of berries the next morning, you're back on your way.

You're very relieved to finally meet up with an Israelite scout. He is as glad to see you as you are to see him!

"King David has been worried about you," he reports.

The scout leads you to the army's camp where a few men are immediately assigned to escort you back to Jerusalem to see David. You leave early the next day and find yourself sitting at the side of David by nightfall.

"I was so worried about you," he admits. "It's really a relief to have you back again!"

As you talk with your friend, you find that Hanun has captured the rest of the men and dishonored them by cutting off their beards. David tells you that these men are now in Jericho until their beards grow back.

Just a few days after you return, Joab, the general who is leading David's army against Hanun, sends for David's help.

"I want to help, too," you tell David, but he insists that you stay in Jerusalem and rest.

David takes a large army with him and easily defeats Hanun's men, even though they've hired foreign soldiers to fight with them. Soon David is back in Jerusalem. He tells you about a promise he made to Jonathan: to show kindness to his children. David says he wants to fulfill that promise.

"I must find out if any of his sons or daughters are still alive," he says.

David searches out Ziba, an old servant of Saul's. Ziba, in turn, leads him to Meribbaal, Jonathan's only remaining son. When David's men find Meribbaal, David gives him all of the land that belonged to his grandfather, Saul. After David has honored his promise to Jonathan, things quiet down and return to normal.

One day, however, David meets a beautiful woman named Bathsheba and he marries her. Before long, they have a son. Everything seems to be going well and David looks happy. Then, unexpectedly, your friend becomes very sad.

"What's wrong?" you ask.

"I have sinned," David replies, "and now the Lord is punishing me by sending sickness upon my son."

"I don't understand," you say. "What are you talking about?"

"I wanted to marry Bathsheba so badly," David sadly explains, "that I had her husband Uriah sent into battle to be killed."

You're very shocked by this news. Even though you feel sad when David's son dies, you're so upset by David's actions that you decide to return home to Bethlehem for a while.

In a few weeks, you find yourself back in the same field where you and David used to watch sheep. You sit down to think. You spend a lot of time thinking during the next few months. Then one day you have a visitor. It turns out to be Absalom, one of David's older sons.

"I noticed how upset you were with my father, and I have an offer to make to you," he says. "I know that I would make a much better king than my father, especially after what he has done, and I would like your help."

Though you have always liked Absalom, and are still upset with David, you're not sure whether to accept his offer or not.

If you help Absalom try to overthrow David, turn to page 66.

If you want to stay with David, turn to page 77.

"You're a fine man Absalom, and you'd make a good king," you reply. "I would be glad to help you in any way I can."

"I knew I could count on you!" he says approvingly. "I won't need your help right away, but I'll send for you when the time comes."

Absalom leaves, and life in Bethlehem goes on as usual. Every now and then, David sends messengers with his request for you to return to Jerusalem. But you never respond. You continue to honor your commitment to Absalom.

One day a local farmer returns from Jerusalem where he had gone to settle a dispute with one of his neighbors.

"The king had no time to spend with me," he complains, "but his son Absalom helped me. That boy would make a wonderful king."

Hearing this makes you wonder how Absalom is going about trying to become king. When other neighbors go to Jerusalem and return with the same story, you realize what's happening. Absalom is treating the people kindly, not because he really cares about them or wants to help them, but because he wants them to prefer him to David and make him king.

If you disagree with Absalom's methods and want to try to warn David, turn to page 68.

If you are still very upset with David and wish to stay with Absalom, turn to page 70.

Though you may still be upset with David's actions, you don't approve of the way Absalom is lying to the people of Israel. You try to get a good night's sleep so you can leave for Jerusalem first thing in the morning.

When you reach Jerusalem, you see Absalom at the front gates of the city. He is talking to un-suspecting people about their problems. He stops you as you pass by.

"What are you doing here?" he demands.

"I don't agree with your dishonest methods of winning people over to your side," you reply qui-etly, "and I've come to talk to your father David about you."

"I won't allow it!" Absalom snarls.

"You can't stop me!" you answer firmly as you walk away, more determined than ever to warn David of Absalom's bad intentions.

You take a room at an inn to lie down and rest after your long journey. As you drift off to sleep, you hear a noise. Before you know it, someone has crawled through the window of your room, but you pretend to be asleep. Then you realize that the in-truder is not after your belongings…he's after you! Overpowering you, the man quickly secures a strip of heavy cloth over your mouth, knotting it to keep it tight. As he ties your hands and feet together, you realize that you were wrong about Absalom. He can stop you.

The End

Though Absalom's ways seem to be deceitful, you're still so shocked at David's actions that you decide to stay with his son.

A long time passes before Absalom is actually ready to overthrow his father, King David. But, when the time comes, you're right there. You meet Absalom at Hebron, where he's beginning to gather an army. When he has enough soldiers, Absalom spreads the news throughout Israel that *he* is now king. Though this is not true, it's still enough to make David flee from Jerusalem.

"We can now take the city for ourselves," Absalom tells his followers. And the next day you do just that.

By the time you arrive in Jerusalem, Ahithophel, one of David's counselors, has betrayed him and come over to Absalom's side. You are there when Absalom announces that he'll be leading his army across the Jordan River to battle David's forces. You offer to accompany him.

"Perhaps you're too old to go into battle," Absalom replies. "But you could be a great help if you would stay behind and supervise the rest of the troops."

You think about this and realize that you're really not as quick as you used to be. This could prove a dangerous disadvantage on the battlefield. The choice is yours.

If you accompany Absalom into battle, turn to page 72.

If not, turn to page 74.

"I'll accompany you to the battle," you tell Absalom, "but I'll stay behind the line of fighting to help treat the wounded."

"Good," he says.

You soon find yourself crossing the Jordan River with Absalom's army. You are on your way to the city where David's army is encamped. When you reach some woods just outside the city, the soldiers set up camp and you find yourself a spot in a small medical tent.

Before you realize it, Absalom's army is marching toward the city. David's troops are already heading your way. Soon the battle is underway and casualties from Absalom's army begin pouring in.

After long hours of treating injuries, you decide to step outside for some fresh air. As you sit at the base of a tree, you suddenly feel rough hands grabbing you. You're now a prisoner of David's soldiers! *Maybe,* you think as they take you off to their camp, *maybe this is what I deserve for refusing to forgive David and turning against him.*

The End

"I agree," you say to Absalom. "I am too old to go into battle, but I'd be happy to help by staying in Jerusalem."

"Thank you," he replies. "Your help is greatly appreciated."

With that, Absalom leads his army across the Jordan River to fight David. For the next few days, you await word of the battle, but there's no news. Then, as you're eating breakfast one morning, a messenger comes riding full speed into the city.

"Absalom has been defeated!" he shouts. "David is once again king of Israel!"

I must apologize to my old friend, you think.

Later in the day, David arrives in a procession with many happy people singing and dancing alongside. You wait until things have calmed down before approaching David. Though you must spend two days outside the city, you're finally able to meet with David privately.

"Please forgive me," you say. "I made the mistake of believing Absalom's deceitful words."

"I don't see how you could have ever doubted me," David replies with tears in his eyes. "But, I ask the Lord to help me to forgive you just as he has so often forgiven me."

You say good-bye and return to Bethlehem feeling very sorry for having betrayed your oldest and dearest friend. You can't seem to forget David's sad eyes. You pray that he will be able to forgive you.

Back in Bethlehem, you take a long walk. You come to the field where you first met David so many years ago. You sit down in the tall grass. Leaning back against a large rock, you look up. The sky above is clear and blue. Everything is peaceful. You hear again, in your imagination, the words of one of David's beautiful prayer-songs:

> "I look to the hills!
> Where will I find help?
> It will come from the Lord,
> who created the heavens and the earth.
>
> "The Lord is your protector,
> and he won't go to sleep
> or let you stumble.
> The protector of Israel
> doesn't doze
> or ever get drowsy.
>
> "The Lord is your protector,
> there at your right side
> to shade you from the sun.
> You won't be harmed
> by the sun during the day
> or by the moon at night.
> The Lord will protect you

and keep you safe
from all dangers.
The Lord will protect you
now and always
wherever you go."

I'm sorry for my sins, Lord, you pray in your heart. You close your eyes and smile. You know God has heard your prayer.

The End

"I'd never even think of betraying David" you tell Absalom, "and I'm shocked that you, his own son, would!"

You quickly leave for Jerusalem to try to warn David of his son's plan. When you arrive there a few days later, it's very late. *I'll see David in the morning,* you decide as you settle down at an inn. Not long after, someone knocks at your door. It turns out to be an old friend of yours and David's.

"I heard that you had returned," he says. "David will be very glad to see you."

"And I'll be just as glad to see him," you reply. "But I'm afraid I have some bad news."

You go on to explain Absalom's plan and his offer to you. Your friend thinks quietly for a moment, then shakes his head slowly. "Don't tell David about this," he advises. "He loves his son so much. Let's just hope that Absalom will abandon this terrible plot."

You agree with this reasoning and, when you see David the next day, you say nothing about Absalom's plan. Instead, you enjoy a happy reunion, and David invites you to stay with him in Jerusalem for as long as you like.

The days pass and you almost forget about Absalom's threat. But one day Absalom announces that he's going to Hebron to keep a vow he's made to God. You're almost sure that he's really preparing to try to overthrow David, but you still say nothing. As it turns out, you're right.

Two days later, a messenger hurries into Jerusalem. He shouts the news that most of Israel has turned against David and gone over to Absalom. Just as you thought, David is shocked and hurt. When David hears that Absalom is heading toward Jerusalem with an army, he and his whole household, along with six hundred loyal soldiers, flee Jerusalem for nearby Mount Olivet.

When you reach the mountain, David receives word that Ahithophel, one of his chief counselors, has also gone over to Absalom's side. Hearing this, David calls for his other counselor, Hushai.

"I want you to go to Absalom and pretend to be on his side," David instructs Hushai. "You can then give him bad advice."

When you hear this, you think that you could possibly be of help by accompanying Hushai. This would be a way to personally teach Absalom a lesson—but it could be dangerous.

If you ask to accompany Hushai, turn to page 79.

If not, turn to page 84.

"I'd like to go with Hushai," you tell David.

"It could be dangerous," he replies, "but, if you really want to, I'm sure Hushai will welcome your help."

"Yes, I want to go," you insist.

You soon find yourself back in Jerusalem where you and Hushai are able to convince Absalom that you are both on his side. While Hushai offers Absalom military advice, you simply become a follower, doing odd jobs and continually trying to steer Absalom away from David.

While you work quietly in the background, Hushai is able to convince Absalom to accept his advice rather than that of Ahithophel. Because of this, Absalom prepares his men to cross the Jordan River to fight David's army. This is when you begin running into some trouble.

It seems someone has overheard you talking with Hushai and has found out that you're still loyal to David. Thankfully, this man doesn't suspect that Hushai is also loyal to David, so your plan is still safe. The man threatens to report you to Absalom unless you pay him a bribe. You don't have the money he's asking for and you begin to panic. You're able to stall him by explaining that you're trying to get the money. But you must do some-thing—and quickly.

If you attempt to save David by trying to capture Absalom yourself, turn to page 81.

If you try to escape and return home to Bethlehem, turn to page 83.

You decide to try and save David by attempting to capture Absalom. The night before he is to fight against David, you get your hands on a knife and some rope. Your plan is to wound Absalom slightly, only enough so that you can bind him with the rope. Then, with the help of Hushai and other men loyal to David, you will bring him to the king under cover of night.

Once darkness has fallen, you pretend to be a messenger in an attempt to see Absalom privately.

"I'll take the message for him," says an army captain when you approach Absalom's tent. "He's busy right now."

"I was instructed to deliver the message to Absalom *personally,*" you insist in a commanding tone of voice.

"Very well then. Follow your orders," the officer says as he walks off.

You're almost positive that Absalom is alone. But, when you draw back the tent flap, you discover two guards dozing. It would be foolish to try and carry out your plan now. Absalom sees your look of uncertainty and catches the gleam of your knife in the candlelight. He immediately understands your intentions. "Seize him!" he cries. The startled guards spring to their feet. Within seconds, they're upon you.

You are now the prisoner. You have no idea what will happen next, but you are at peace. You know that you've tried your best to defend your friend David.

The End

After making your decision, you plan your escape. You'll wait until nightfall when no one will notice you. Then you'll simply ride off on one of Absalom's mules and return to Bethlehem.

As the sky darkens, you saddle a mule and set out. A sentry stops you as you leave the city, but when you tell him that you're running an errand for Absalom, he allows you to pass. From there, you ride until you reach a small village just outside Jerusalem where you spend the night.

It takes some time to reach Bethlehem. When you finally arrive, your family and friends gather to welcome you. Everyone is eager to hear about your many adventures with David.

You settle down in your old home. Word soon reaches you that David's army has defeated Absalom. Though you keep in contact through messages, you are too old to visit David. You live out your life where it began, telling stories of your great friend, David, to everyone who will listen.

The End

Even though you're tempted to get back at Absalom for hurting his father so much, you realize that this would be wrong, so you decide to stay with David.

As Hushai heads back toward Jerusalem, David leads his followers farther away. Though it seems like an eternity, Hushai is finally able to get Absalom to accept his advice. He convinces Absalom to wait until he has a bigger army to fight an open battle with David. Then Hushai sends David an urgent message instructing him to hurry and cross the nearby Jordan River.

With that, you and all of David's followers make a quick night crossing of the river, putting more distance between you and Jerusalem. It's not long before you come to Mahanaim, a city where all the people are still loyal to David. They give David, you, and the men plenty to eat and drink.

The next morning you wake to find Absalom's army waiting in a nearby forest. David's army now includes extra men from the small towns you passed through as you fled Jerusalem. The army soon begins its march out of Mahanaim. David wants to go with his soldiers to meet Absalom's troops, but the officers persuade him to stay in the city. You decide to remain behind with David.

After a while, a messenger comes running toward the city.

"Tidings, my lord the king!" he shouts. "The Lord has avenged you of all those who rode up against you!"

Though everyone is thrilled at the victory, David begins to cry when he learns that his son Absalom has been killed in the battle. When they see the king mourning, David's soldiers feel ashamed of their victory. After Joab speaks with the king, David apologizes and joins in the celebration.

All of you march happily back to Jerusalem. The whole city is bursting with joy as David returns to his throne, singing a song of thanks:

"You reached down from heaven,
and you lifted me from deep in the ocean.

"You rescued me from enemies, who were hateful
and too powerful for me."

Because David is getting older, his assistants now run the country. During this time, David completes his plans for his son Solomon to build the temple of God when he becomes the king.

Even though it's David's wish that Solomon become the next king of Israel, he soon learns that

Adonijah, another of his sons, is planning to become king. However, David has his most trusted servants anoint Solomon with oil, making him king of Israel.

You spend the rest of your days living peacefully in David's palace, helping him to raise money for the temple. You thank God for having let you spend so much of your life at the side of your friend, David, a great hero of Israel.

The End

BOOKS & MEDIA

The Daughters of St. Paul operate book and media centers at the following addresses. Visit, call or write the one nearest you today, or find us on the World Wide Web, www.pauline.org

California
3908 Sepulveda Blvd., Culver City, CA 90230; 310-397-8676
5945 Balboa Ave., San Diego, CA 92111; 858-565-9181
46 Geary Street, San Francisco, CA 94108; 415-781-5180

Florida
145 S.W. 107th Ave., Miami, FL 33174; 305-559-6715

Hawaii
1143 Bishop Street, Honolulu, HI 96813; 808-521-2731
Neighbor Islands call: 800-259-8463

Illinois
172 North Michigan Ave., Chicago, IL 60601; 312-346-4228

Louisiana
4403 Veterans Memorial Blvd., Metairie, LA 70006; 504-887-7631

Massachusetts
Rte. 1, 885 Providence Hwy., Dedham, MA 02026; 781-326-5385

Missouri
9804 Watson Rd., St. Louis, MO 63126; 314-965-3512

New Jersey
561 U.S. Route 1, Wick Plaza, Edison, NJ 08817; 732-572-1200

New York
150 East 52nd Street, New York, NY 10022; 212-754-1110
78 Fort Place, Staten Island, NY 10301; 718-447-5071

Ohio
2105 Ontario Street, Cleveland, OH 44115; 216-621-9427

Pennsylvania
9171-A Roosevelt Blvd., Philadelphia, PA 19114; 215-676-9494

South Carolina
243 King Street, Charleston, SC 29401; 843-577-0175

Tennessee
4811 Poplar Ave., Memphis, TN 38117; 901-761-2987

Texas
114 Main Plaza, San Antonio, TX 78205; 210-224-8101

Virginia
1025 King Street, Alexandria, VA 22314; 703-549-3806

Canada
3022 Dufferin Street, Toronto, Ontario, Canada M6B 3T5; 416-781-9131
1155 Yonge Street, Toronto, Ontario, Canada M4T 1W2; 416-934-3440

¡También somos su fuente para libros, videos y música en español!